THE CASE FILES OF DETECTIVE STEPHEN TABELING

BLACK OCTOBER

AND THE MURDER OF STATE DELEGATE TURK SCOTT

BY STEPHEN TABELING & STEPHEN JANIS

Copyright © 2020 by Stephen Tabeling & Stephen Janis

All rights reserved. No part of this publication may be reproduced, distributed, or transmitted in any form or by any means, including photocopying, recording, or other electronic or mechanical methods, without the prior written permission of the publisher, except in the case brief quotations embodied in critical reviews and other noncommercial uses permitted by copyright law.

ISBN: 978-1-953048-57-8 (Paperback)

The views expressed in this book are solely those of the author and do not necessarily reflect the views of the publisher, and the publisher hereby disclaims any responsibility for them.

Writers' Branding
1800-608-6550
www.writersbranding.com
orders@writersbranding.com

CONTENTS

CHAPTER ONE: BLACK OCTOBER AND
THE MURDER OF TURK SCOTT.............................1

    AN UNWIELDY CASE AT SUTTON PLACE 4
    THE DRUG BUSINESS COMES OF AGE 7
    THE LAW AND THE CASE.............................. 11
    OUR FIRST CLUE..................................... 14
    THE STRANGEST SEARCH 17
    TWO STORIES, SAME SEARCH.......................... 19
    A TRIAL WITH TWISTS 21
    BLACK OCTOBER......................................26

CHAPTER TWO: GAMBLING ON
PENNSLYVANIA AVENUE 28

    INTERNAL AFFAIRS....................................33
    SURVEILLANCE..35
    THE DISAPPEARING WARRANT 40
    About the Authors...50

CHAPTER ONE

BLACK OCTOBER AND THE MURDER OF TURK SCOTT

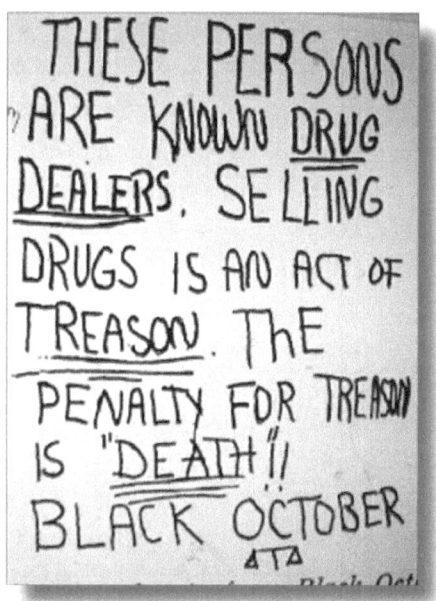

Baltimore City, like most communities, has a split personality.

Within its borders, alleys and back-ways two parallel worlds exist side by side. Distinct civic selves, which become self-evident if you spend enough time immersed in both.

I know this because I was… and still am, a cop.

During my career as a Lieutenant in Baltimore City Homicide, I often worked at a crossroads where the two worlds met. At the point where healthy productive communities and the criminal element clashed.

And while I worked dozens of murder cases and headed a variety of investigations, there is one case that to this day stands out as emblematic of the split personality that characterizes this town.

This case defined just how destructive the burgeoning drug war in Baltimore was to become; and just how complicated and costly fighting it would be.

It was a case that pitted the city against itself, and revealed how scars of divisive racial mistrust would be slow to heal — if ever they would heal at all.

It was a case that has all but been forgotten, although it sowed the seeds of many of the problems that hamper the effectiveness of our justice system even today.

It was also a story of a social movement that threatened to engulf the city in civil war, a vigilante movement which still remains in part, a mystery.

I'm talking about the murder of Maryland State Delegate Turk Scott.

For most of my career I was an investigator, a detective, a person whose beat was the juncture of the aforementioned divide between the healthy and the unhealthy.

And when it came time for me to do my job, I tried, for lack of a better analogy, to be precise, and dogged. I mean methodical, hard-nosed, but within the law. I didn't fight violence by abandoning the law; indeed, I embraced it. I was "the law," so I acted like it. But I also acted within it.

That's been the mantra of my career — to follow, teach, and learn the law; it's the only way to police effectively.

To insure that cops remain peacekeepers and community builders, simply demands they follow the law. Because when your job is to literally stand on the precipice of communal dysfunction, the law keeps the chaos at bay.

That's why the law has evolved. That's why it has to be followed. And in the murder of James "Turk" Scott, it was all I had.

AN UNWIELDY CASE AT SUTTON PLACE

It's a strange life, being at the nexus of all things violent. In the City of Baltimore, which numbered almost a million people when I was a homicide investigator, if someone found a body with a bullet hole in it they called us.

This is why a ringing telephone on the floor of the homicide division always had a sinister undertone. Like a perversion of Zuzu's wing-earning angels, when the bell chimed in our office, it meant someone had just met a violent end.

And if that call was from a homicide detective who was already on the scene of a murder to tell me I needed to "see this," I always knew there was something extraordinary attached to the body that lay prone and lifeless in some back alley or on a sidewalk in the city's urban hinterlands.

But nothing really prepared me for the murder, and its aftermath, that began with an early a.m. Friday the 13th phone call from one of my detectives who was standing in the parking garage at the Sutton Place Apartments on that morning in July, 1973.

It was a grisly scene, yes.

A middle-aged African-American male lay on the parking garage floor surrounded by at least a dozen shotgun casings and spent slugs. The victim was dressed in a beige suit and paisley tie; blood-spotted entry wounds were visible on both his chest and lower leg.

But what caught my eye that morning, and what would ultimately draw this case into a firestorm of controversy was something else. Something you rarely see at a crime scene. I guess you could call it a message of sorts… and it wasn't subtle.

Strewn about the body like leftover litter from a raucous Irish wake were leaflets — dozens of them. All emblazoned with the name of a group that we had recently become aware of, but at that time had few clues to just how violent it would become.

Black October.

We didn't know much about the group at the time. Only vague rumors of a Westside-based vigilante movement that was targeting drug dealers. A phone call to the editor of the *News American* and *The Sun* that a drug dealer had been murdered. Gunned down because he was poisoning the city.

But Black October was not my only concern. Because the murder victim sprawled on the floor of the parking garage was also a well-known public official — as I said before, State Delegate Turk Scott.

He was a politically connected bail bondsman, a consummate Baltimore insider who had been appointed to a seat in the Maryland General Assembly just months before.

And the plethora of shell casings scattered across the pavement made one thing clear, the killers were not simply trying to ambush the 48-year-old politician as he exited his car.

No, they had something entirely different in mind.

It appeared the killers were trying to send a message.

Scott had recently been indicted by federal authorities for drug dealing: one count for conspiracy and three counts for distribution of heroin by attempting to bring 40 pounds of dope into the city. An indictment that made headlines across the country regaling the tale of a public official who was alleged to have been involved in the business of moving drugs through the City of Baltimore.

It was a drug case that confirmed everything I had suspected about the burgeoning and insidious illicit-narcotics business that was infiltrating the upper echelons of the city's political class. It was a growing underworld of incestuous relationships I had discovered while detailed to a special Narcotics Task Force in the early 1970s (which I will say more about later).

There, lying on the pavement, his tie flipped over the back of his head lapping at the spent shotgun shell casings that crept around his body like dead bugs, was the best example of what the growing influence of the drug trade had wrought: An elected official gunned down in broad daylight.

And then there was the note from Black October.

Scrawled on the 8-by-11-inch sheets in brutish handwriting was the name of a group that had been lurking in the shadows of the city's undercurrent of violence. A loose organization that was rumored to be waging a vigilante war against the drug dealers in the city but whose real intentions remained as murky as the drug business they were alleged to be fighting.

It was group that we had heard of, but knew little about.

Allegedly named after an organized effort during the Vietnam War to aid heroin-addicted African-American soldiers, the group had come to our attention when another suspected city drug dealer was gunned down in broad daylight. Several days after that murder someone claiming to represent Black October called the *News American* newspaper and said the dealer was the first victim of their nascent war against drug dealers.

"He was killed because he was a drug dealer," the caller was quoted as saying.

And now inscribed on the sheets of paper strewn across the parking garage was a short but succinct threat, a posthumous death sentence for Turk Scott and a warning of more trouble to come:

"These persons are known drug dealers," the flyers proclaimed. "Selling drugs is an act of treason. The penalty for treason is 'death'!! [signed] Black October"

THE DRUG BUSINESS COMES OF AGE

As I said before, my job was to investigate murder, crimes of passion, dispassion and plain old vengeance. Baltimore City, as most people well know, has a penchant for violence.

People get killed violently for a whole variety of reasons. But in the 1970s, as I'm sure is true today, much of the killing was related to the business of selling illicit narcotics: drug dealers killing drug dealers.

And I had a unique perspective on not just why, but *how* drug dealing was becoming the most destructive crime pattern in Baltimore.

Because before I was assigned to the city's homicide unit, I was the only Baltimore City police officer tasked to the city's first special Narcotics Task Force.

Formed in 1971 by then-State's Attorney Milton B. Allen, the Task Force was designed to combat the growth of the organized drug business in Baltimore.

Our job was not just to arrest drug dealers, but to accumulate intelligence about the organizational structure of the business as a whole. We were tasked with fleshing out the big picture and identifying the major players.

And during a span of a few short years we did exactly that.

One of the biggest challenges we faced fighting drug dealers in the late 1960s and early 70s was keeping up with the growth of the organizations that had evolved hand in hand along with increases in the trade of drugs like heroin, cocaine and marijuana. As the drug trade expanded, so did the organizations.

But we needed intelligence, a clear and useful picture of who ran the drug business in Baltimore.

To achieve this we collected arrest data from the city's nine police districts and various narcotics units, and created a telephone tip line to receive information on drug dealers from the general public.

We also set up wiretaps and surveillance; we followed the players who soon emerged as the top organizers of the city's growing drug trade.

And through this work we were able to assemble a pretty coherent picture of how heroin and cocaine made its way from international locales to the streets and neighborhoods of Baltimore. And what we learned, which has been kept secret for decades, was pretty ugly.

It was ugly because in the 1970s, put simply, the heroin trade was not fronted by underground organizations or petty thugs. No. Thanks to our intelligence- gathering efforts we knew the exact opposite to be true.

The first thing to understand is that Baltimore was a major market for heroin even back then.

We didn't have estimates, but based on the size of some of the biggest local drug organizations, kilos of dope were being moved into the city on a daily basis. It was quite a bit of product, product that needed to be cut, packaged, and distributed every day.

The person who pushed product into the Baltimore supply chain for many of the organizations we tracked was a New York-based dealer named Gary Matthews.

Matthews was one of the biggest heroin traffickers on the East Coast. A legend, in fact, who gained notoriety by circumventing the Italian Mafia to buy heroin directly from the Cubans and Colombians and sell it in at least 20 cities up and down the East Coast.

Matthews would be what we call today a kingpin; he had the ability to deliver weight. And as his ability to import drugs directly to the East Coast grew, he found a ready market in Charm City.

We observed him in the company of some of the city's most infamous drug dealers, including "Little Melvin" — Melvin D. Williams, who played The Deacon on the TV show "The

Wire" — and a man named Big Head Brother, who I will say more about later.

But what we learned from watching Matthews work, and how his supply was moved through the city, said quite a bit about how the drug business was changing — and the City of Baltimore along with it.

Because in the late 1960s and early 70s the drug business in Baltimore began to shape the urban landscape we see today.

The change was not simply in the obvious unsubtle exodus of residents that would begin a long, unending decline in population, nor the wholesale desertion of downtown — a fate the recently deceased Mayor (and later Governor) William Donald Schaefer spent his entire career trying to reverse by building lustrous Inner Harbor pavilions, stadiums at Camden Yards, and other tourist attractions.

The change perceptible on the street level, in the neighborhoods, was from an unseen tide of despair that began to slowly wash over once stable communities in the form of a deviant and destructive business that had taken root in areas where the factories and jobs had left.

It was, in short, the ascent of organized drug dealing, and in particular heroin, that had begun to spread its deadly tendrils throughout the city. With it came the steady erosion that would soon begin to take apart Baltimore's bedrock of middle class communities piece by piece.

The growing business of distributing opiates gained momentum in the early 1970s and began the inevitable decline that has left us with the urban wasteland we see today.

To be sure, there were plenty of other factors that contributed to the urban decay that has become as legendary as Maryland's signature crab cakes. Unscrupulous landlords and blockbusting real estate speculators combined with the wholesale withering of the city's industrial base. And of course the simmering racial tensions between white and black residents that has always defined, in part, the city's psyche.

But the often destructive business that began its unabated takeover of Charm City was perhaps the strongest symptom of the sickness within. And it was my job as a detective in the Baltimore Police Department to fight it.

Unlike the seemingly more chaotic drug business of the new millennium, the process of dealing heroin in Baltimore City was not only well-organized in the early 1970s, it was also ingrained in the fabric of the community via legitimate business owners, and to be sure, a well-known soon-to-be-gunned- down politician at Sutton Place.

This I learned not only as the lead investigator of the special Narcotics Strike Force, but also as a homicide investigator for the city police department.

Through our work at the Narcotics Task Force, we had identified the command structure of multiple drug organizations in Baltimore City, traffickers that ran their operations from legitimate businesses.

Like the heroin ring at the Penn-Dol Pharmacy on Pennsylvania Avenue, for example. Or the drug gang headed by the owner of the Bear's Den on the 2800 block of Greenmount.

What was true then, and may well be true now, is that the business of drug dealing existed like a shadow cast over the everyday life of inner city Baltimore. It was like a subcutaneous infection, something that is in plain sight but stealthily hidden at the same time.

Still, it was the Turk Scott case that brought the ever-lurking business of illicit narcotics and its insinuation into the fabric of city life to the fore like never before. It was in a way emblematic of what we had learned in the Narcotics Strike Force:

The drug business was now the city's business.

THE LAW AND THE CASE

There is one thing you learn rather quickly investigating homicides: Everything changes when the case goes to trial.

It doesn't matter how solid a case you build, how many witnesses you find or how airtight the forensic evidence is. Once you enter a courtroom, your case is fair game. Defense attorneys and even the press can transform a straightforward case into a set of seemingly implausible facts.

This is why it is so vitally important for police officers to understand the law. If you don't know the law, you can't make the case.

Be careful of putting too much credence in the idea that law is an obstacle, a set of rules that gets in the way of rightfully prosecuting criminals. It's just not true.

Life is often messy, crime is virtually always messy. Think about, when someone picks up a gun, points it at a human being and fires, what's left is a mess, blood and guts.

Something police call a "crime scene."

But the law is a way of taking something that is complicated and messy and giving it some sort of organizing principle, a structure for piecing together all different elements of a crime into a coherent case that gives the prosecutor the best possible chance of winning a conviction.

That's why the law is important, because it more often than not makes sense. And that's also why I've spent a lifetime since I retired as a Baltimore City police officer to teach it to as many officers as I can.

Because in the end, no matter how careful you are, when you end up in court, anything can happen.

I know it for a fact, because I've been there.

As I implied at the beginning, the killing of Turk Scott was nothing short of an execution, which we figured out quickly how the killers got done. But even as the case was coming together — I didn't know at the time — how we solved it would come under assault in ways that would overwhelm what we had uncovered.

The first thing we noticed was two distinct types of bullets: shotgun shell casings and spent slugs that, as I said before, surrounded the body.

The slugs appeared to be .38-caliber, the shotgun casings, 12-gauge.

In all, we found about half a dozen shotgun shell casings and half a dozen spent slugs from the .38. It seemed that there might have been two shooters.

Next we examined the body, an examination that confirmed my initial impression that the shooter, or shooters, had more in mind than simply killing Scott.

You see, when you shoot someone in cold blood, depending on the motive, you stop when the victim appears to be dead; it's only common sense.

But in the Scott case, the gunman, or gunmen, didn't.

Scott had wounds all over his body, including several in his back, one near his kidney, which more than likely killed him, one in his chest, and one in the lower leg.

But when we removed his shirt, we found yet another gunshot wound at the base of his neck — more than likely a wound inflicted after he was already dead. The number of bullets and the postmortem wounds made it clear, the killers were sending a message.

So now we had an execution style slaying of a public official who was under indictment for drug dealing. Further complicating the case, the specter of Black October loomed. What if, I thought at the time, this group really was preparing to wage war against drug dealers in the city? What if this was just the first in a series of planned killings?

To be sure, whoever was behind Black October wanted us to believe that Scott's murder was just the beginning.

So when a man claiming to represent the organization called the *News American* and took responsibility for the killing, we knew we had to solve this case quickly, otherwise whoever or whatever Black October was, could mushroom into something far worse.

OUR FIRST CLUE

Fortunately it didn't take long to get our first break in the case.

As I said previously, the crime scene was littered with Black October flyers that linked the murder of Scott to their war against drug dealers. But it was not just the flyers that gave us the lead we needed.

Not far from Scott's body, lying near a stairwell in the garage was a rolled up *News American* newspaper. From the start of the investigation it caught my attention not because it was odd for someone to toss a newspaper on the ground in a parking garage, but because it was slightly rolled in a way that could be used to conceal a weapon. As we canvassed the scene, our crime lab technicians took it, along with several flyers, for analysis.

And sure enough, just a day later they found prints. Seventeen points on the newspaper and 30 points on one of the Black October flyers.

Not just anyone's prints however, but 17-point handprints of someone well known to me and other detectives: A young, man who was connected to one of the city's most powerful African-American families and who I had encountered several years before.

Sherman Dobson.

Dobson was not your average suspect — hardly.

He was the son of a minister and nephew of one of the most prominent African-American pastors in the City of Baltimore, Rev. Vernon N. Dobson, a Baptist minister and civil rights activist whose reputation extended well beyond Charm City.

His family lived in Ashburton, the most upscale African-American neighborhood. They had influence and power. The type of influence and power that black churches wield in Baltimore, then and now.

I had encountered Sherman six years earlier in the most unlikely place, in the cafeteria of a city high school.

It was a steamy afternoon in 1967 when I was working plainclothes in the Northern District. I was called to a disturbance at Baltimore Polytechnic Institute, which in 1952 had become the first public high school in the city to racially integrate its student body. More than 200 students were staging a "sit-down" to protest against the Vietnam War. We were called in to calm things down.

But as I and another city police officer entered the cafeteria, the students locked the doors. Suddenly we found ourselves trying to mitigate tensions inside a claustrophobic school lunchroom filled with unruly teens.

One of the leaders of the student protest was Sherman Dobson. He was obviously bright, and certainly had the other students under his sway. He approached, catching me off-guard by instantly giving me a nickname.

"Hey! Clark Kent," he called to me as I stood in the cafeteria. (I never did find out precisely what he meant by calling me by Superman's alter ego, although some people say I looked a bit like the comic book character back then.)

We managed to persuade the students to ratchet down the protest, but my encounter with Sherman stayed with me.

And now we had his fingerprints on at least two pieces of evidence from the Turk Scott crime scene.

Plus we uncovered even more evidence pointing to Sherman.

Witnesses said they saw two men lingering near the parking garage just before Scott was gunned down. But they also reported seeing a red Royal Cab driving from the scene after Scott was shot.

And that got our attention.

That's because not one, but two cab drivers had reported being hijacked by three masked men in and around the Ashburton area in the days leading up to the shooting. One kidnapped days before the shooting, and the driver of another Royal Cab the same morning Scott was shot.

Even more intriguing, one of the drivers, who we believe was carjacked as part of a practice run several days before Scott was killed, got a good look at one of his captors.

The driver told us he picked up three young men in the 900 block of Druid Hill Avenue near Druid Hill Park and that once inside the cab the three men brandished weapons and forced him to drive to a deserted area of the park.

There, the trio forced him out of the cab and handcuffed him to a tree. Fortunately for us, one of the assailants stayed behind while the others took off with the cab. Later, the driver said he could identify the kidnapper who stayed behind.

One of my detectives created a photo array for the cabbie, an array which later would become a basis for an appeal of a conviction stemming from the driver's kidnapping, an array which included Sherman Dobson.

And sure enough, the cab driver identified the man who watched while he was handcuffed to a tree as none other than Dobson himself.

THE STRANGEST SEARCH

Remember at the beginning of this story I said that everything changes when a case goes to trial?

It's a statement born out of experience.

We had evidence, hard evidence that implicated Sherman Dobson. Fingerprints from two pieces of evidence found at the murder scene and a solid identification by the cab driver who had been carjacked at gunpoint just days before Scott was killed.

With this evidence, and a tip from an informant that Sherman kept an array of weapons at his family home, all we needed was to conduct a search.

One of the most important and least understood aspects of any investigation is the obtaining of a warrant and the conducting of a proper search. The Fourth Amendment to the Constitution protects us from unreasonable search and seizure. It is a logical and productive safeguard.

A safeguard that has to be respected.

Yet quite a few cop shows these days try to depict the Fourth Amendment as an obstacle, something that prevents police from catching criminals, or provides lawbreakers with a myriad of technicalities to evade punishment.

However in my opinion, as a lifelong police officer and experienced investigator, nothing could be further from the truth.

The Fourth Amendment not only protects citizens, it protects police as well. Imagine if we could simply barge into any home or open any door in a non- emergency situation without so much as a calling card. That we could simply stop people on the street whenever we felt like it, or break down the doors of people's homes simply because we didn't like them.

That's what life would be like without the Fourth Amendment. The police would be hated and feared by everyone, with no cooperation, and with good reason.

But there's more.

Writing a search warrant is not only a requirement of the law, it is a task that ultimately makes for a stronger case. It helps cops organize their thoughts and evaluate evidence before they go knocking on a door, a vital step in case building that makes us better prepared when we finally go to trial.

Remember, in order to preserve citizens' individual freedom to move about, or right to come and go as they please, there has to be some protection in place to ensure it.

A cop with a gun and a badge is an ordinary person with extra-ordinary powers. If he or she could stop you without probable cause or enter your home without a warrant signed by a judge, it would make the core right of democracy — the freedom to come and go as you choose — impossible.

Also, and almost as important, it is really not that difficult to persuade a judge to sign a warrant. In my career I was never turned down, in part because several well-respected judges took the time to teach me how to write a proper warrant.

And never were those lessons more important for me than in the case of Sherman Dobson, because the search that we executed during our investigation ended up consuming the case at trial and having a pivotal impact upon the outcome.

With the evidence we had and the tip from the criminal informant, we didn't have any trouble obtaining a warrant from the judge. The only thing I was worried about was that Sherman would get wind of our plans and hide the evidence.

Fortunately that did not happen.

TWO STORIES, SAME SEARCH

When we knocked on the door of the Dobson home in the heart of Ashburton in Northwest Baltimore, it was the estimable Rev. Harold Dobson, Sherman's father, who answered the door, with Sherman's uncle Vernon in tow.

"I have a search warrant," I told the reverend. "And we're going to search the house."

Both men were polite and respectful. In fact, Rev. Vernon Dobson escorted me through the house personally as I conducted the search.

Just for the record, I had roughly seven officers with me, two other detectives and four uniformed cops.

Inside a closet in Sherman's room we found a .38 caliber handgun and ski mask.

Downstairs in the basement we found a shotgun hidden behind a shelf. And we found shotgun casings and bullets for both guns. It was certainly enough evidence to raise serious questions about Sherman's involvement in Turk Scott's killing.

We handed over the guns to the Crime Lab. But after a series of ballistic tests, our technicians concluded that neither of the weapons could be linked to the shell casings found near Scott's body.

Nevertheless, while we were not able to connect either of the guns to the shooting, our search would certainly have implications for the case, which I will delve into later.

Still, armed with the fingerprints and the cab driver's identification, we were able to get a warrant for Sherman Dobson's arrest.

When he arrived on the homicide floor, he was his usual confident self. He took one look at me and said, "I remember you, Clark Kent." But that was all he said. Before I could even ask what he meant by the nickname or have a polite conversation with him, he had a lawyer.

Still, even with a suspect in custody and what seemed like a pretty solid case, I knew we were in for a rough trial. When you arrest a member of one of the city's most prominent African-American families, a son and nephew of two preachers, you're going to have a fight on your hands.

Little did I know it would be a knock-down, drag-out brawl.

A TRIAL WITH TWISTS

Looking back on the trial of Sherman Dobson, former city prosecutor Milton Allen, Maryland's first African-American state's attorney, had a simple lament about the price he paid for the drama that unfolded inside Baltimore's Clarence M. Mitchell Jr. Courthouse in 1973.

"Steve, the Dobson case cost me the election," he lamented years later. (Allen was defeated for reelection in 1978 by William A. Swisher, who four years afterward was himself defeated by later Baltimore Mayor Kurt L. Schmoke.)

It was a time of exacerbated racial tension in Baltimore in the decade following the assassination of Rev. Martin Luther King Jr., a period when blacks and whites alike retreated to their own neighborhoods as they had in the years preceding integration.

I think Allen was right. In a sense, the trial of Sherman Dobson was a watershed moment for the city's criminal justice system, a notorious case so thick with politics it was hard to breathe in the courtroom. Because from the onset of the trial the defense made it crystal clear that the defendant, Sherman Dobson, wasn't the one who was on trial at all. It was in fact us, the Baltimore City Homicide Division. I'm not overlooking the fact that our work, to a certain extent, is always on trial. But in this case the defense took that strategy to an extreme that I have never experienced before or since in all my years as a cop.

Let me say before I go any further that I respect the decision of the jury in the Dobson trial, along with the right of a man accused, to defend himself. Everything I write here is a matter of fact reported by the media and recorded in court transcripts. My only complaint is I believe politics overwhelmed the proceedings to the point that what went on in court had very little to do with the evidence against Sherman Dobson, and everything to do with painting the Baltimore Police Department in the worst possible light.

When I say politics, I mean the tensions between the Police Department and the community. That's because it was the dramatic testimony of Sherman's uncle, Rev. Vernon Dobson, that turned the proceedings into an indictment of us, the cops. An entirely different version of events told in open court which still puzzles me to this day.

Reverend Dobson's testimony centered on our aforementioned search of his home just before we charged and arrested Sherman. But what he told the court had little resemblance to what I did that evening.

Instead of the four uniformed officers and two detectives accompanying me that evening, Reverend Dobson said there were over 150 cops stationed outside his Ashburton residence long before we entered.

And instead of what I recall as an orderly search of his residence in the presence of the reverend the entire time, he told the jury a "pug nose" officer had run up the stairs to Sherman's bedroom.

Even more astounding to me, was Reverend Dobson's claim that we had broken into the basement before knocking on his front door, and planted guns in the cellar. Kind of ridiculous, given that the guns we allegedly planted turned out to have nothing to do with the case.

But the strategy behind all this appeared to be conflicting testimony that was pretty easy to figure out.

To say that the atmosphere in the courtroom was tense would be like saying that standing on the corner of Biddle and Gay Streets in the middle of a hot August afternoon is a little "uncomfortable."

Not only did the supporters of the Dobson Family pack the courthouse daily, the press touted headlines each and every day of the trial. So as the Rev. Vernon Dobson sat on the stand accusing us of planting evidence and of showing up like a small army on his front lawn, the accusations made headlines, and the headlines weren't good.

Never mind that his testimony conflicts with what I believe happened, which was a perfectly legal and orderly search.

That wasn't the point.

What Reverend Dobson's testimony accomplished was to put the focus on us, not his nephew. And it was a strategy that paid off.

Because for nearly half a day I was on the stand. Sitting in the witness box, I had to read the run sheets for uniformed officers and patrol cars for every single district in the city to recount what every officer was doing. Every call for service, every dispatch, every movement of a patrol car, all to disprove his claim by showing that it just wasn't possible 150 officers could have been standing outside his house.

So there I sat for hours reading one activity sheet after another as the jury seemed to melt into a semblance of disinterested boredom. One by one, I read off the calls for service, car stops, and other mundane deployment details. Hour by hour I recounted the whereabouts of each and every police officer that donned a uniform that day. Minute after minute of tedious testimony, sitting in the witness stand, grilled by the prosecutor, poring over run sheets while the jury sat stupefied.

But in the end, it didn't matter.

Even though one of the cab drivers identified Sherman as his kidnapper, and even with the expert testimony from our Crime Lab technician that proved the prints on the newspaper and Black October flyers found at the scene were Sherman Dobson's, a Baltimore City jury found him not guilty of killing Turk Scott.

And while he was found guilty of kidnapping and robbing the city cab driver who identified him, the verdict in the killing of Scott was a stunning blow to justice in this city. And I say that not just because I worked on the case.

Sherman Dobson was a troubled youth, dangerous to himself and others.

Several years after he was acquitted of Scott's murder he shot a police officer in Baltimore during a robbery. The officer survived, but the fact remains that Dobson was willing to point a gun at a cop, and at least in that instance, fire.

But what made me most uneasy about Scott's murder trial was the role politics played in its outcome.

As a cop I understand how politics influences what we do, how sometimes the will of an aggrieved constituency influences the process of policing.

Guilt or innocence is often a matter of perspective. Even the worst criminals don't think of themselves as bad, or even at fault. And even when evidence is solid, and proof hard to refute, personal prejudice can often trump the facts.

But there is a time for politics and a time to mete out justice. In the process of deciding guilt or innocence the meddling of politics that has nothing to do with guilt or innocence can render a justice system dysfunctional.

Ultimately the jury acquitted Sherman, and in the end I can't argue with a jury. But I think the acquittal was more a rejection of police tactics, not the evidence itself.

Which is why I focus so much of my attention on the law. Why I spend so many hours learning it and teaching it to other cops. It's like an insurance policy for justice. If you want to insure that personal prejudice and partisan politics cannot corrupt the process of deciding right and wrong, follow the law.

Somebody killed Turk Scott, a man who was not a stellar citizen. In fact, he represented the deepest and most troubling form of corruption. The kind of rot from within I believe stunts the efforts of honest, hard working city residents to turn Baltimore back into a thriving, industrious metropolis.

Let's remember the system was working when Scott was gunned down. The feds had Scott under indictment. He was facing serious charges. More than likely, he had stopped dealing drugs.

But his murder was vigilante justice, nothing more. An act that sounds good in theory until someone with a gun shows up on *your* doorstep to act as judge, jury and executioner.

People that kill without compunction are dangerous. They do not discriminate. That's why this murder needed to be solved, for the good of the community, for the protection of everyone.

But in the courtroom, the good of the whole was not served, in my opinion. Guilty or not, politics won out, and a police officer later had to pay the price for that lapse in communal judgment with a bullet in his chest.

Dobson appealed the kidnapping verdict. He argued that the photo array was prejudiced because he was the only suspect in the array wearing glasses.

The appeals panel sent the case back to Circuit Court for a new trial; however the state chose not to retry it.

But the more important effect of the outcome of the trial is best expressed in Milton Allen's lament — that he lost his next election because of this trial. In other words, for pursing justice, he was turned out of office. Since then, the much more politicized State's Attorney Office has struggled to right itself.

And what of Black October? If their motive really was to rid the street of drug dealers, did they succeed?

BLACK OCTOBER

No, they certainly did not succeed, and for a very simple reason.

Violence, no matter the intent behind it, doesn't heal. In fact, it only creates new wounds, new cases that have to be pursued, and a new batch of bodies in the morgue.

I can't say I blame the black community for feeling besieged by the growing tendrils of the drug trade. I can't even say I blame the people who lived with the ever growing disruption of an increasingly entrenched drug business for trying to take matters into their own hands, if that's what Black October was really all about.

I don't blame them, but I certainly can't condone it.

Because there was something else lost as a result of Scott's death that never made headlines. Secrets untold that show why vigilante justice is not only morally wrong, but ineffective.

Scott never had his day in court.

In other words, the person who could have shined a light on the cancer of corruption the drug business was inflicting upon the city's productive community never got to testify. The opportunity to expose how the city's criminal element was infiltrating Baltimore's power structure via the drug trade ended with a dead body in a parking garage.

Even after Scott's murder people I knew at the FBI wouldn't talk about the case. Whatever secrets he had he took to the grave.

To be sure, Scott was not the only suspected drug dealer Black October took credit for murdering. Shortly after his death the group claimed killing two other known dealers. The city was, to say the least, on edge.

So the police had to act: We identified at least six people who we believed were involved with the group and put a 24/7 tail on them. We didn't have enough evidence to bring charges; the intent was simply to let them know we were watching.

After several weeks of surveillance the young men we believed were involved in the Black October killings disappeared. I know it sounds odd, given that we were watching, but one by one they slipped away and vanished, and never returned to Baltimore, at least not on my watch.

Afterwards, the killings stopped, and Black October seemingly ceased to exist.

I often think about the case, about Turk Scott and the secrets he left behind on the floor of that parking garage. I think about it because I witnessed a piece of Baltimore history that to this day remains unresolved in my mind.

Like so many of the cases I worked on and recount in this book, the criminal side of Baltimore's psyche won a partial victory simply by silencing Scott.

True, people went to jail; and true, Black October's campaign of vengeance ceased. But in the end, we never heard from the man who knew the truth. Our community never had the chance to cauterize the wound that the drug business was inflicting upon the city by outing him.

By making him talk, by learning the truth, maybe we could have struck a serious blow against it.

It was an opportunity lost.

I guess I'll just have to live with that. But what bothers me even more, is... so will the people of Baltimore.

CHAPTER TWO

GAMBLING ON PENNSLYVANIA AVENUE

Take it from me, there's nothing more complicated, exhausting — and risky — than investigating other cops.

Imagine for a minute, that your boss came to you with information that co- workers were breaking the law. Imagine if he or she then asked you to investigate their crimes and build a case against them.

Sure, it sounds intriguing, maybe even exciting to someone who has never done it.

But being the bad guy isn't fun; in fact, if you're the cop going after other cops it can be downright dangerous.

One thing you learn quickly as an investigator is that no one wants to get caught. And if the suspects have a gun and a badge, they can sure enough make it harder for you to catch them.

And that's not even accounting for the well known fact that investigating cops is a quick path to occupational isolation and inevitable institutional blowback.

But that doesn't mean it's not important. In fact, in my opinion, as a society, how we police ourselves is a good indicator of how effective a police department will be in general.

That's because cops who don't follow the law aren't very good at enforcing it.

And therein lies the rub.

How do you police people with guns and badges? How is it possible to create an enforcement mechanism that can get past the insular relationships and tight-knit community of cops to ferret out the bad ones?

It's not easy, to say the least.

That's why when I read the statement in the downtown chambers of the Baltimore Criminal Justice Commission in the spring of 1966, I knew I was headed into a world of trouble.

Cop trouble, the kind that hits you across the forehead. A sense of foreboding that percolates in the mind, an instinctive sixth sense that makes you naturally wary of a potential career-ending mess.

And by the time I finished reading the statement of the woman who recounted how Baltimore City police officers were involved in the numbers racket, I knew the end result of the case before it even began.

Like I said: Trouble.

I had been called to the offices of the Baltimore Criminal Justice Commission in 1966 by one of the best legal minds in the city, now-retired Court of Special Appeals Judge Charles E. Moylan.

Judge Moylan, who was then City State's Attorney, had gathered several high ranking law enforcement officials there at the behest of a reporter from the *Baltimore Sun*. The reporter had apparently stumbled onto evidence that several city police officers were involved with a large numbers operation on Pennsylvania Avenue.

Evidence in the form of a witness.

When I arrived, I sat down to read the witness's statement in the company of Judge Moylan, Ralph Murdy, a former FBI agent who was head of the commission, interim Police Commissioner George Gelston, and an ambitious *Sun* reporter.

It was an odd group to say the least.

The witness told us about her knowledge of a relationship between a powerful cop and a suspected numbers man named Phil Taylor who worked an illegal lottery operation at 1500 Pennsylvania Avenue: home to a barbershop, hotel and eatery, and also, according to the witness, a sizable numbers business.

But it wasn't the tale of the gambling operation that gave me pause. No, it was something that sparked the feeling of foreboding every cop develops over the course of his or her career.

Call it a survival instinct.

I think any police officer, particularly an investigator, will understand when I say that the longer you wear the uniform you either develop an extraordinary sense to sniff out trouble — or you soon find yourself working security in a parking garage. I'm not talking about the standard bad-guy-with-a-gun trouble. No, that comes the minute you put on the uniform.

I'm talking about the ability to see the shit before it hits the fan. The aforementioned sixth sense that tells you the situation you're wading into is going to get you into trouble that will require a crowbar to pry you out of.

It's like witnessing a car accident in slow motion, you see two vehicles on a collision course long before they arrive at the point of impact.

I know this sixth sense and I believe in it because when I was called to that meeting downtown in the Criminal Justice Commission's office, I recognized from the minute I sat down in the chair and read the witness statement that whatever they were about to ask me to do would probably not end well for me.

I'm not trying to give away the story, or add a touch of fatalism to the investigation I am about to recount; instead I'm trying to give you a sense of what it feels like and what it really means to be an investigator.

That is, the implications of looking into the soul of a city that I knew from experience had an uncanny ability to compromise the law in the pursuit of vice.

I had worked plainclothes and developed a pretty good sense of how money from illicit businesses like prostitution and gambling found its way into the coffers of seemingly legitimate enterprises. So I knew at that moment, that delving into this crime would put me on an island of sorts, a friendless way station where you have few friends and plenty of enemies.

Let me explain why.

There was an alleged numbers man who our witness knew was making payoffs to a then unnamed high level Baltimore City police officer, a man who the witness said had the power to make things "go away."

And that's when the sixth sense kicked in. I mean, it's pretty obvious that investigating a police officer is not a choice job. It's almost a cliché to say that working the 1966 version of internal affairs was not a way to win friends and get promoted. However it wasn't cops going after cops that made me wary.

What my sixth sense told me, was that if a high ranking officer was involved, then quite likely a whole bunch of other people with influence, connections and ways to make an investigator's life miserable could also be on the take. And that is why I knew I was in for it.

Still, even though I had my doubts, what could I really say? Judge Moylan was a mentor, one of the best legal minds in the city who taught me both respect for and how to use the law effectively. Plus the case was the type of challenge that a good investigator lives for.

And maybe, to be honest, it was the type of case *I* lived for. Who knows what drives a person to do things that you know may end badly? It's sort of like career vertigo, you want to jump in feet first even though there is nothing but hardening concrete that awaits you.

So I said Yes. And as it turns out, I was an idiot.

INTERNAL AFFAIRS

Remember that in 1966 the Internal Affairs Division was a new idea, so cops weren't used to being watched. In fact, there was little if any independent oversight of the department.

And then of course, you have the simple fact that everyone loves to gamble, and a whole lot of powerful people love the profit it generates.

At that time the city was awash in numbers: illegal lotteries that worked just like the current legal version, just a little less conspicuous. In fact, it wasn't until 1973 that the state created its own lottery, a move that was the beginning of the end for the illegal numbers business.

But at that time, if you wanted to buy a lottery ticket, the numbers racket was your game. You can imagine given the hundreds of millions of dollars the state rakes in currently year in and year out, that even then it was a big business.

A business I was about to wade into in search of a crooked high-ranking cop, no less.

But back to the case.

As I said from the outset, the cast of characters I met at the Criminal Justice Commission was hardly your typical investigation team.

For one thing, the *Sun* reporter had taken the unusual step of bringing the witness to us in the first place. And now he wanted to be involved in the investigation — not necessarily standard procedure, to say the least.

Let's face it, the goal of a cop and the job of a reporter are often at odds. I have a lot of respect for the First Amendment, but a criminal investigation is something to write about *after* the fact, not during.

However since the reporter effectively brought the case to us, he wanted in, and he got his wish. The next sticky question was operational. How would I conduct an investigation of high-level cops without someone getting wind of it?

We hatched a plan whereby I would be quietly detailed to a private detective agency in Roland Park. The idea was for me to simply fade away: I couldn't tell anyone what I was working on, not even my supervisors.

Basically, I was on my own. And whatever happened in the course of this investigation, the blowback would be on me.

Welcome to the world of the investigator.

And so, with little fanfare, one witness and a reporter in tow, I began to work on a case that would not only shake the department to its core, but even prompt significant changes to the way we did business.

SURVEILLANCE

So a few weeks later I found myself in the offices of the International Detective Agency, an outfit run by a former army intelligence officer named Marshall Myers.

Detailed to me were two city cops, one who I will call "Sam," a cop who would become a major thorn in my side later on.

The evidence outlined in the witness statements was a start, but not nearly enough.

The first witness had provided a sketchy link between cops and gambling on Pennsylvania Avenue: She had worked for a numbers man named Phil Taylor. And while she was not directly involved in the operation, she was close friends with Taylor and thus had overheard details of his wheeling and dealing, details that piqued my interest.

While she didn't want to specifically talk about cops being involved in illegal lotteries, she did know that Taylor was making payoffs to several officers, including one who lived in Baltimore County and drove a nice car, and whose house had a swimming pool.

The payoffs were big, she said. One month's worth of bribes would be enough for her to live comfortably on for a year.

In fact, this witness told the commission she was sure police were involved in the illegal lottery business, but that there was little point in reporting crooked cops because too many were involved.

However she was not the only witness who had firsthand knowledge of police involvement in lotteries, specifically the Pennsylvania Avenue operation.

After talking to several other witnesses, the same two names kept coming up, a lieutenant and a sergeant in the Detective Division.

And there was one witness in particular who had quite a story. Her name was Ida May Pryor, a middle aged woman from East Baltimore.

According to the statement she gave us, one night the lieutenant and sergeant showed up at her house with a box. Her daughter answered the door, and called Ida May downstairs because she mistakenly thought the cops had brought them some food.

But it turned out the duo had nothing of the sort. Instead, they stormed into the house and started rummaging through the Pryors' freezer. Ida May asked the sergeant — |whose name was Riggs — if he was in some kind of trouble.

"No," Riggs said. "I just need you to hold something for me," he explained.

It turns out that "something" was roughly $12,000 cash and a box of numbers slips, the take from a day of illegal numbers running down on Pennsylvania Avenue.

He didn't offer any explanation as to why he needed to stash the lottery receipts in her refrigerator, after which he simply disappeared.

The two men also asked if her daughter had bought a number, #541.

"Yes," she told them.

Had it been paid off, one of the detectives asked?

"No," she said.

And then things got really odd.

Not only did the duo talk to her about the cash, but they said they thought Willy Diggs and an associate named Salisbury should pay off on the number, a total of 12 grand. They said it was the only way to maintain their reputation in the numbers business. One of the cops even threatened to hurt Diggs if he got his hands on him.

It was enough to suggest the officers weren't investigating Diggs, but were working in the same business.

And who were these two police officers with what appeared to be a stake in the numbers racket?

It was the very same lieutenant and sergeant that had been mentioned as being on the take by several other witnesses: two high ranking officers from the Detective Division who appeared to be knee deep in the numbers racket.

The investigation into the Western District supervisors progressed, so we began regular surveillance of the 1500 block of Pennsylvania Avenue.

Unlike tracking down drug dealers or other types of low level criminals, when you go after cops you have to be cautious. First of all, cops know all the tricks of the trade, so trying to infiltrate a criminal enterprise run by police is pretty risky business.

That's why we decided consistent surveillance of the location was our best option.

Using two vans equipped with 8-millimeter movie cameras, we parked with a good view of the entire block. We watched and we filmed.

Let's just say it didn't take long for us to get a real sense of what was going on.

From morning until evening every day a lawyer's office and a bar called the York Hotel were awash with people — not just ordinary citizens but cops as well.

In and out all day, the officers and a veritable Who's Who of the city's underground gambling racket were seen entering and leaving the buildings where the lotteries were run.

We couldn't see exactly what was going on inside, but even from our vantage point on the street we could see paper slips being exchanged hand to hand — lots of them.

In my first intelligence report to then-Captain Vincent Gavin, we counted roughly 167 people entering the York Hotel and Snack Bar in less than two hours. I reported that the traffic was so heavy on the block that it was hard to get descriptions.

One of those 167 people was a man known as Mickey Mixup, a well-known lottery lieutenant for Julius Salisbury, the man who was technically responsible for the paying of the #541 ticket belonging to the daughter of our witness.

We also noticed there was an ebb and flow to the traffic: heavy in the morning until noon, and then resuming heavy from two in the afternoon until five o'clock. In between, the foot traffic could be counted on a single hand.

So in my report, I made it clear we believed that these locations were being used for an illegal lottery operation, a conclusion I immortalized in a memo to Captain Gavin several weeks into the investigation.

Meanwhile, the *Sun* reporter was asking for a wire so he could follow what he described as a hot lead. According to him, a gang member working out of Baltimore's red light district known as The Block was helping the cops stash some of the gambling proceeds.

But despite giving him full support and backup his so-called leads typically turned up nothing but dead ends. The key witness or the groundbreaking statement was always just around the corner, he would say. Not a single statement or witness he promised to deliver ever materialized during the investigation.

So I started to believe the reporter was playing us, or else he was trying to keep us interested in what he had to say in order to maintain the inside scoop on where the investigation was headed.

I discussed my suspicions with Commissioner Gelston and told him in no uncertain terms that I thought the reporter was a threat to the investigation. In short, I wanted to put a tail on him.

Gelston agreed.

So I assigned two of my men to follow him — and it didn't take long to get results.

Just one day later my two cops watched as he engaged in a fairly intricate sex act with one of our original witnesses.

Sitting in a car under JFX Rte. 83 not far from the offices of the *Baltimore Sun*, the blissfully unaware reporter seemed to be having an extremely intimate relationship with the woman whom he brought to the Justice Commission just a month before.

And not only did we catch them in the car, but later we observed him entering her home early the next evening and then leaving the following morning.

I reported the dalliance to Commissioner Gelston, who quickly arranged a meeting with the reporter's editor at *The Sun*. Needless to say the reporter soon vanished. I don't know if he was fired, transferred or what, but the man never showed up asking questions again.

His foibles however were just a minor distraction to our case. Surveillance was paying off. We had pretty much established the fact that Pennsylvania Avenue was the central headquarters of a large illegal numbers operation. Even better, with the testimony from Ida May we were on the way to linking the operation to the lieutenant and sergeant from the Detective Bureau.

In fact, we had caught a number of cops from the Western District leaving and entering businesses on Pennsylvania Avenue which served as the apparent logistical headquarters for the illegal lottery.

So with the evidence from surveillance coupled with several strong witness statements, we asked for and received the approval of State's Attorney Moylan to construct a warrant.

Now if you recall, at the beginning of this chapter I mentioned that I knew going in that this case was bound to be trouble. I had an investigator's premonition that things were going to fall apart.

It was not long after I wrote the warrants to search the businesses along that active stretch of Pennsylvania Avenue, that they did.

THE DISAPPEARING WARRANT

It all started with the catchphrase that was my unofficial career mantra. I would employ it with mindless repetition to get it through the thick skulls of cops: how important it is to learn, know, and follow the law. Something I repeated so many times at the city's Police Training Academy, cadets accused me of having dementia: Get a warrant, get a warrant, get a warrant.

With more than enough evidence that the 1500 block of Pennsylvania Avenue was a mecca for illegal numbers, I began to write the warrants for searches on several businesses where we had observed excessive foot traffic, the mercurial characters slipping in and out like ghosts, and the constant shuffling of slips of paper from hand to hand.

As I will discuss later in the book, at that time there was no formal training for Baltimore City police officers with regard to writing warrants. In fact, 1966 was the first year that we had what is known as in-service training — time taken off the beat to brush up on things like the law, though the law was hardly the central focus.

Most of what I learned about writing warrants I learned from judges like Charles Moylan. And now I had to write one hell of a warrant, because I was about to walk into what I assumed from my investigation were some pretty well-connected businesses.

This dilemma, having to learn one of the most basic skills of criminal investigations on the fly, is one of the reasons I'm writing this book. There is a more detailed chapter on the law later in the book but there is no better teacher than a real-life example. This case is definitive of how important a well-written warrant can be.

Any good defense attorney will go over the warrant with a fine tooth comb, looking to find factual errors, for example. Or in some cases, nullify an arrest simply because you didn't have a warrant in the first place.

If he or she is successful, then all the evidence you discovered and confiscated, and all the ensuing leads you developed from the search can technically be tossed out the window. If your warrant or your search is no good, you are going to have trouble.

Of course, that's not what happened in this case. It was in fact worse.

As I stated before, I wrote warrants for several businesses on the block where we had observed and filmed the heavy foot-traffic and the slips of paper exchanging hands.

Just before the raid I received an unusual order from Captain Gavin: he wanted me to use the Western District Plainclothes Squad to conduct it.

I was a little taken aback.

First of all, the Western District Plainclothes Squad was run by a lieutenant who I didn't think would take kindly to being ordered around by a sergeant. Second, some of the men in the squad were caught on our surveillance footage of the block. In other words, some of the same cops who might be the target of our investigation would be taking part in a raid to uncover evidence of their misdeeds.

Remember when I said at the beginning of this chapter that this case would be trouble?

Of course, I didn't have a choice. Following orders is not optional in the Baltimore Police Department, even when the orders are misguided. (You can choose to disobey an *illegal* order, but I'll discuss that in my chapter on the law.)

So there I was, standing in the parking lot of the old Memorial Stadium with a truck, a set of freshly written warrants, and the entire Plainclothes Squad of the Western District standing around scratching their heads.

Since I already knew some of the officers in the squad could be at least tacitly involved in these gambling operations, I knew it was possible they would be tempted to tip off the numbers businesses we were about to raid. So I didn't tell them anything about where we were headed before they were all sitting in the truck and the doors were locked.

Fortunately there were no cellphones in those days.

Now I can't exactly describe how the men looked when I passed around the warrants. Let's just say the term "pale as a ghost" doesn't do it justice. I mean, at that moment they held in their hands warrants to raid several illicit numbers businesses which some of the same men in the truck had been visiting regularly.

Contributing to their evident dismay was the fact that the warrants described how we knew the targeted establishments were home to illegal lotteries — the surveillance film.

So needless to say it was not a happy crew assembled in the truck headed toward one of the biggest search and seizure raids of my career.

But little did I know how the unhappy few would strike back.

When we arrived on Pennsylvania Avenue the officers disembarked from the truck and spread out over the block like a flock of angry seagulls. Then, as the cops entered the businesses to execute the warrants, people from all the shops began to file out onto the street, bewildered.

It wasn't an unruly mob, just a large crowd of customers, office workers, and of course the dumbfounded numbers men. They seemed unable to reconcile the fact that the same police department which had been up until now buttressing their illegal gambling operation was now rummaging through their files and gathering evidence to put them in jail.

I can't say that I witnessed any direct confrontations between my men and the suspects, but I'm sure there were plenty of awkward moments when a cop on the take ran headfirst into one of the people who were paying him off.

Fortunately the raid was successful and we gathered lots of evidence. We pulled boxes of the number slips and receipts.

We found cash and records indicating that the 1500 block of Pennsylvania Avenue was indeed a numbers racket mecca.

Things were looking up, at least for a couple of hours.

But shortly after the raid was concluded, and I started to collect the original warrants, that's when things began to fall apart.

When a police officer conducts a raid of a home, business, or any other space where the Constitution requires we obtain legal permission to enter, the officer leaves a copy of the warrant at the location and brings the original back to the police district where the raid occurs. The warrant is then filed away in a drawer to be presented in court at trial, a practice which actually changed later on because of what happened next.

So after the raid was concluded I did what I always do, gather the original copies of the warrant for the court file. The only problem was, one of the officers, "Sam," said he didn't know where the basic warrant was.

"What do you mean you don't have the warrant?" I remember saying to Sam a bit heatedly standing on Pennsylvania Avenue. But he just shrugged his shoulders and stared up at the sky.

Let me be clear here that warrants aren't something a cop misplaces like a set of car keys or a wallet. When you're conducting a raid it's the most important item in your possession, even more so than your gun. An entire case, including all the evidence collected, can hinge on conducting a proper search.

Any proper search begins and ends with a warrant.

So when Sam stood on Pennsylvania Avenue claiming he lost the warrant, I was not only dumbfounded, I was beyond angry. I knew he was trying to set me up. Not only that, he was showing complete disregard for the law.

Realizing then that this could screw up the entire case, I immediately called State's Attorney Moylan. He too was outraged. So outraged, in fact, he called the police commissioner and asked that Sam be fired.

But that was just the beginning of the treachery.

Unknown to me at the time, one of the men from the Western District Plainclothes Squad who assisted me in conducting the raid was caught counseling suspects on prospective lawyers.

It was unreal.

So here I had one cop hiding a warrant and another trying to give suspects tips on how to beat the rap.

But at least the raid produced evidence — solid evidence.

In one barbershop we confiscated slips containing 19 bets at $4.25 a pop. In another we found 112 numbers for bets totaling $79 and another box of slips with 160 bets and $131. In a bar entered by Sam and another plainclothes officer, more betting slips and cash were discovered.

But the cop who accompanied Sam also said he thought he saw a plainclothes officer sitting next to one of the suspects, an officer who apparently slipped out the back door before anyone bothered to question him or let me know about it.

The alleged cop slipped out before the warrant was served to suspect James Jackson Jr., who was coincidentally holding roughly $2,600 cash and corresponding betting slips.

Five suspects in all, including Jackson, were charged. But it was the disappearance of the warrant and the cast of characters who made an appearance on our 8-millimeter films that turned this case into a high and holy mess.

While we were preparing for trial, the word got out that it was none other than the original two, the sergeant and lieutenant whose "repo" job was to get back $12,000 in cash captured on our surveillance footage.

And they weren't the only ones.

Three other Western District officers starred in the film, along with two corrections officers and a probation agent. It was, to say the least, a broad spectrum of representatives from law enforcement.

The raid netted enough evidence to charge five men with running an illegal gambling operation, but the police officers were another story.

Shortly after the raid the lieutenant retired, and just before I was about to interview the sergeant, I was ordered by newly named Commissioner Donald Pomerleau to drop it.

It was not an enviable position to be in. I'd just caught a bunch of cops more than likely committing crimes. I was now the face of an investigation that had revealed an ugly truth about the City of Baltimore: the cozy relationship between cops and the city's illicit gambling business.

And now, as I predicted, I was being prevented from finishing the job. But it would get worse.

The trial for the five men was a big media event. Not only because we'd busted a pretty large numbers operation in the heart of the city or because five well-known numbers runners were facing serious criminal charges.

What made the trial big news was who wasn't on trial, which was the elephant in the room that drew everyone's curiosity. It was the cops caught on film and the rumors that police were involved but never fully investigated, which made the trial more than a local curiosity.

Remember, I stated earlier in this chapter that I could smell trouble when this case was first presented to me. And it was one of my own men who threw the first proverbial punch, absconding with the original warrant. But nothing prepared me for what happened next.

The day I was scheduled to testify I had brought a copy, not the original, of the warrant with me. It was the best I could do because the original had never been found.

The prosecution team knew that the defense would make an issue of the fact that the original warrant was missing. I was simply hoping that a copy would be enough.

But believe it or not, before I could finish my testimony about our surveillance and the raid, the copy of the warrant — which had been sitting in the jury room — went missing.

It's hard to believe that a warrant on an explosive case like this would be stolen not once, but twice. And who would commit such a brazen act? All I know to this day is that there were six cops in that jury room, six suspects. Even today I don't know which officer stole it.

But then things got really strange.

Outside the courthouse, a reporter from *The Sun* approached me.

"I know what happened to your warrant," he told me.

"Well then, tell me," was all I could say, not believing that once again a *Sun* reporter was knee deep in my case.

"Ask my editor," he replied.

So during the lunch break I made my way over to the *Sun* headquarters on Calvert Street, a few blocks north of the courthouse.

The meeting didn't last long: "I'm not going to tell you how I got it, but I have your warrant," the editor told me.

I couldn't believe it, there in his hand, was the original warrant I had given to Sam just before the raid. The missing warrant which had thrown a monkey wrench into the biggest case of my life had somehow ended up in the offices of a newspaper.

We didn't exchange but a few words, I was due back in court.

Once I arrived I quickly found Moylan told him what happened. He was, to say the least, dumbfounded.

"Where the hell did you get that?" he asked, completely baffled by the sudden turn of events.

"From an editor at *The Sun*," I told him.

I do have some idea how the warrant got into the hands of the media, but it's hearsay and I can't prove it, so I don't want to detail it here.

The truth is, the fact that the warrant ended up in the hands of a reporter rather than a cop tells you something about this case, and the city itself.

Obviously there were police involved in the illegal gambling, in other words committing crimes serious enough to warrant an in-depth investigation. But in the end, the corrupt forces inside the department won out.

And to a certain extent even though we recovered the warrant and presented it in court, the damage had already been done.

Initially we thought we would have to prosecute the case without the original warrant, and so the prosecutors decided to show the film of Pennsylvania Avenue during the presentation of their case. It was a tough call because that evidence tipped our hand and let everyone know what we knew.

Although I was sequestered while the film was shown in court, I was told you could see the shadows of people leaving the courtroom as their images were projected onto the screen.

Yes, we had solid proof that corruption was a serious problem inside the police department. Yes, we had evidence of ongoing illegal activities of a number of law enforcement personnel. But that's not what the court ultimately focused on.

In the end, after the five men were convicted, Judge Joseph P. Carter asked Commissioner Pomerleau to conduct an internal investigation into the disappearance of the warrant.

Pomerleau then told the press he would look into — and I'm quoting directly here — "all aspects or integrity, or lack of integrity, on the part of police officers."

And guess who he focused on? Me, of course.

As I said at the beginning, I knew in the end that this investigation could turn back on me in a heartbeat.

Given that cops and influential people were involved, and that money and gambling was fueling it, there was no doubt I was in trouble.

It really wasn't a surprise to me then. When you seek out the truth in a community where the truth is unwelcome, there's bound to be a reaction. Many times during my career I was criticized for not knowing when to stop. And this was one of the investigations where it seems I didn't.

The fallout was, of course, swift.

A major who didn't like me was put in charge. After I filed my report on the missing warrant he created a list of a hundred questions about the investigation and the missing warrant that I had ordered.

Truthfully it seemed like a trap; the wording and the language were too precise.

So I secretly obtained counsel, answered each question in sequence, and carefully.

It infuriated the major, who accused me of consulting a lawyer. Which of course I did.

On the surface I was investigated for failure to manage my troops; for losing the warrant, and also for not keeping a closer eye on Sam.

But in the end, I was simply a scapegoat for the ugliness that a jury and a room full of top brass couldn't handle.

Someone had to take the fall for the ugly picture of policing presented in that courtroom, and it was me.

Eventually I was cleared of any wrongdoing. But that didn't stop Pomerleau from calling me every name in the book as I sat in his office just a few weeks later. It was an hour-long tirade during which he questioned my character, integrity, and ability, using expletives as adjectives.

"You will never work in plainclothes again," he promised. His concession was to allow me to choose the district where I would be working as a sergeant in uniform.

His tongue-lashing was one of the most humiliating experiences of my life. Afterwards I remember one of my mentors, Captain George Duechler, who was present during Pomerleau's tirade, asking me how I could just sit there and take the abuse.

I simply told him I had four children and a wife to take care of. At the time I had only a seventh grade education, and policing was something I was good at.

But that doesn't mean I wasn't angry. Or that adversity doesn't sometimes reap rewards.

Maybe that was the moment I decided to go back to school, a decision that would not only lead to obtaining the high school diploma that I lacked, but a college degree, a master's, and several advanced certificates that I will discuss later in the book.

Maybe it just taught me a lesson that when you delve into the corrupt sinew of a community, that you're on your own. An investigator, in the end, is really an island unto himself. That when you pull back the curtain on the corrupt elements in society, the person who holds it is often made the scapegoat.

It's like being an unpopular prophet — if people don't like the message, they find ways to discredit the messenger.

But there was something else beneficial about my first wide-ranging investigation of cops.

There was a lesson from the investigation that stuck with me through 50-odd years of law enforcement. A lesson that would get me through the hard times and difficulties of going where no one wants you to go and where no one is willing to face the truth.

It was a lesson that to this day I would share with anyone who walks the path of an investigator.

Wait. Be patient.

Because the tables will turn, as they surely did for me.

About the Authors

Stephen Tabeling was the first detective to win a murder conviction without a body. A cop who investigated the attempted murder of former Mayor William Donald Schaefer. A detective who was on the scene when a sniper shot seven Baltimore police officers in the bloodiest day of violence in the history of the city force.

Put simply, former Lieutenant Stephen Tabeling's history and the history of the city he served are one and the same.

And now the man who started out walking a beat in Northwest Baltimore but later supervised some of the most consequential criminal investigations in the annals of this city is opening his case files, and his conscience, for all to see.

Stephen Janis is an award winning investigative reporter who has worked for newspapers, online watch sites, and television. He won a Maryland- Delaware-DC Press Association award in 2008 for investigative reporting on the high rate of unsolved murders in Baltimore. In 2009 he won an MDDC Press Association award for Best Series for his articles on the murders of prostitutes. As co-founder of the independent investigative website Investigative Voice, Janis's work uncovering corruption and government waste in Baltimore City will be chronicled in the upcoming national documentary "Fit To Print." The site has won worldwide critical acclaim for its unconventional presentation and hardnosed reporting and is read regularly by insiders in city government as well as the police department. Janis is the author of three novels, Why Do We Kill?, Orange: The Diary of an

Urban Surrealist and This Dream Called Death. In addition to reporting and directing content for Investigative Voice he currently teaches journalism at Towson University.

www.ingramcontent.com/pod-product-compliance
Lightning Source LLC
LaVergne TN
LVHW040202080526
838202LV00042B/3276